Henry Mazyck Clarkson

Evelyn

A romance of the war between the states. In verse.

Henry Mazyck Clarkson

Evelyn
A romance of the war between the states. In verse.

ISBN/EAN: 9783337065171

Printed in Europe, USA, Canada, Australia, Japan

Cover: Foto ©Andreas Hilbeck / pixelio.de

More available books at **www.hansebooks.com**

EVELYN;

A ROMANCE OF

"THE WAR BETWEEN THE STATES,"

(IN VERSE,)

WITH AN APPENDIX OF

MINOR POEMS,

BY

HENRY M. CLARKSON, A. M., M. D.

CHARLESTON, S. C.
WALKER, EVANS & COGSWELL, PRINTERS,
Nos. 3 Broad and 109 East Bay Streets.
1871.

EVELYN.

I.

Of wild, of warlike times I tell—long years
Of wavering hopes, and soul-impassioned prayers—
Dark days of deadly strife, and direful hate—
Deep deeds decisive of a Nation's fate.
Too late his tears have dimmed the Southron's eye,
His heart hath heaved too oft the heavy sigh,
Alas! to let these mournful memories die !
   But, sadder yet the subject of my song—
A strange, wild Tale of Grief—of private wrong—
Of spirits brave, defiant of the Foe,
Yet crushed at last, beneath their weight of woe :
A Tale of Love, its tremblings and its fears,
Its thousand tender thoughts, and wayward tears,
Its fond, delicious doubts, its hopes, its sighs,
And all its pleasing, fitful fantasies.

   But turn we, now, to earlier days, ere blood
Had whelmed us with its red remorseless flood.

Not yet the cruel cannon's deafening roar
Had drenched Virginia's soil with crimson gore:
Nor foe had crossed Potomac's peaceful waves,
To make our land, a land of tear-wet graves;
No vandal-tread drew nigh, but far and wide,
His fertile fields the farmer's wealth supplied:
Rich meads of waving grain grew fresh and green,
And Peace and Plenty everywhere were seen.

Where blooms the cypress and the sighing pine,
Where climbs the closely-clinging columbine,
And tall magnolias cast their cooling shades,
Mid myrtle-groves, and greenest Everglades;
Where flowers know not the snowy shrouds of Death
Or icy Winter with his withering breath;
Where perfumes kiss the bosom of the earth,
And Nature smiles, and Beauty owns its birth—
There, on a mild and summer-scented morn,
By Eutaw's banks, was Albert Ashleigh born:
'Mid Carolina's hills his infant eyes
First caught the blue and splendor of the skies.
In Wealth's luxurious lap he lay and smiled,
His yearning parents' first and only child:
Their link of love, their idol, and their pride,
Nor means, nor pains, nor plans were aught untried,

To make him worthy of the name he bore—
As proud a name as Peer or Prince e'er wore.
Of gentle blood begot, this boy, forsooth,
Grew up a goodly and a gallant youth.
  Just at that tender April-time of life,
When Boyhood's heart, with budding feelings rife,
Untouched by care of Winter's later gloom,
Is gliding into youth's soft summer bloom ;
When strange, new sentiments inflame the breast,
And all the senses feel a sweet unrest—
'Twas at such yearning age young Albert met
A kindred Spirit, he could ne'er forget—
A Spirit beaming out from eyes so bright,
The very stars grew pale within their light.
'Twas but a girlish form, but, oh ! so rare
It seemed that Beauty's softest seal was there !
You need but note that face so passing fair,
That warm blue, melting eye, and midnight hair;
You need but note that rich, soft voice, I ween,
That modest grace, yet proud, majestic mein,
The waving music of those accents mild,
To know Virginia claimed that beauteous child.

  Where limpid Massaponax lightly laves
The slopes of Spottsylvania with its waves,

Its trembling waters gliding deep and wide
To wed with Rappahannock's troubled tide,
Upon its banks, embosomed in the wood,
Young Evelyn's cottage-home, Glen Arvon, stood
Neath nodding elms, and maples' silver sheen,
Its ivied porch and graceful gables seen ;
Its gravelled walks, 'twixt turfs of blooming rose,
Its placid look, its lake-like light repose,
Its open, friendly door, its larder stored,
Its hospitable hearth and cheerful board,
Its countless comforts, to the mind suggest
Virginia-welcome to the greeted guest.

Yet, not in this sequestered home, so sweet,
Did Albert and the guileless Evelyn meet,
But far across the hoarse Atlantic's roar
Afar beyond her dear Virginia's shore,
Beneath the blue of love-enkindling skies,
Where love, once born, burns deep, but never dies—
In lands of classic lore and deeds sublime—
Italia's flowery soil and sunny clime.

In Florence, on a summer's afternoon,
One dreamy day of blossom-dropping June,
With thoughtful brow, and kindling eye intent,
A Tuscan painter o'er his pallet bent,

The blended colors on his canvas beamed
With living light.   The blue-veined temples seemed
To swell indignant, and with crimson flush,
To glow beneath the touches of his brush :
Soft smiles, resplendent as the Orient day,
Around the radiant eyes appeared to play,
Anon, to nestle in the dimpled cheek.
As now, the trembling lips would seem to speak,
Or quivering, part, to murmur forth a sigh,
Like silver-toned Eolian melody.

'Twas Leonardo's skill which thus portrayed
This breathing semblance of a beauteous maid,
And long he labored to depict each charm,
Then drooped his head upon his weary arm,
And gazing on the work his hands had wrought,
In vain he strove to crush the rising thought—
One thought indelible, that would not die—
A life-long memory of days gone by—
Till weary Nature, watchful of her claim,
Enrapped in gentle sleep his aged frame.

In dreams he lives his happy childhood o'er,
He looks into his Lucia's eyes once more ;
Nor hears he now the opening of the door,
The studied, noiseless step across the floor,

Nor sees his graceful Pupil near him stand,
Till lightly touched by Albert's friendly hand,
He wakes, and troubled, starting from his dreams,
His gray locks glistening in the sunset beams,
He anxious asks: "And thou art come, my boy!
Hast seen her, Albert, and canst give me joy?
Does Lucia live? Hast left her at Lausanne,
Or lies she ill, a stranger, in Milan?
Go! bring her, boy! Go! tell her she must come
With husband, Evelyn, all, to share my home,
And say, ''tis Leonardo begs the bliss—
The playmate of her girlhood asks her this.'"
    Then answers Albert: " Sir, be quiet now;
Too oft hath fever flushed, of late, that brow;
So come—I pray thee, do not labor late,
Our cariole waits us at the garden gate!"
    "Stay! Albert, I was dreaming, ere you came,
Of days gone by, ere this old shattered frame
Had bent with age. I walked, methought, once more,
A youth, along the Adriatic's shore,
And *one* was with me there, whom, tho' a child,
I vainly loved with love intense, as wild
As those rough waters rushing o'er yon reef—
Arno's rude mockery of mortal grief.
    How oft my hours of boyhood were beguiled

By Lucia's smiles!   And, yet, she never smiled
Whene'er I talked of love!   The years wore on—
Long years to one whose light of light was gone ;
In vain, I worshipped at another's shrine,
In vain, I thought to drown my woes in wine ;
I cursed, at length, my Fate, and followed Fame.
Meanwhile from o'er the seas a stranger came—
A pleasing youth, who won my Lucia's hand,
And took her with him to his far-off land.
He was your countryman, my boy, **and none**
Denied him worthy of the **love he won.**
Full many **a** flying year since then hath past
With Lethe on its wings ; **and** Time, at last,
Hath lightened Disappointment's poignant pains,
And friendship only now for her remains.

   'Tis told that Lucia lived in easy wealth,
Nor lost the beauty of her blooming health,
Till two hard winters gone, a flowery flush
Played o'er each roseate cheek—a **hectic** blush—
The kiss of wan Consumption's wasting breath—
Red, rosy trophies of the conqueror, Death.

   As some fair shrinking bird, in winter-time,
Will seek the shelter of a milder clime,
So Lucia left her home across the sea
For warmer skies—her own sweet Italy.

Her ills beyond the skill of mortal man,
In early spring I saw her in Milan,
Her husband, anxious, bending o'er her couch,
As Evelyn soothed her with her softest touch;
We watched her wasted form and wan white cheek;
Her faint smile made me weep.   I heard her speak
From sweet, pale lips—her lustrous, lovely eye
Illumed with light of Immortality."

As Leonardo turns to hide a tear,
His pupil speaks: "Sir, pardon me, but there
Upon that breathing canvas thou has set
A face, it seems not easy to forget;
The more its faultless, faithful lines I scan,
The more, methinks, I have seen it in Milan."

"Aye, likely boy!   'Tis Lucia's matchless face,
And yet in Lucia now, 'twere hard to trace
The rounded fullness of that girlish grace;
From memory, boy, that beauty I impart,
The fadeless memory of a faithful heart;
'Twas thus she once upon my pathway smiled—
As such I loved her then—a laughing child;
With that sweet face the evening I've beguiled,
And fondly gazing on it, gazing, dreamed—
A sudden, deathly pallor o'er it seemed
To spread—anon, a smile, as angels wear,

In momentary splendor lingered there :
Methought it moved ; and then a whisper said :
' Weep, Leonardo ! for thy Lucia 's dead !' "
  The old man paused, and, sighing, turned away,
As Albert answer made : " 'Twas but the play
Upon your canvas of the dying day—
The flushing of the sunset's parting **beam**—
But then that dream—it seems ' *not all a dream,*'
For yesterday, at fall of eventide,
Thy loved and lovely Lucia gently died."

  'Tis morning in Milan : the great Cathedral's pon-
    derous gate
And iron doors, now harshly on their heavy hinges
    grate :
With muffled, **measured** tread, in **sombre** march, a
    mournful few
Are onward slowly moving thro' the light bespan-
    gling dew ;
A funeral-bell hath early tolled its tones of wild des-
    pair,
Its death-like sullen dirge hath died upon the startled
    air :
The hollow throats of organs peal their brazen notes—
    the while,

A cortege bears a coffined form along the lengthy aisle,
And softly, with the incense, to the stuccoed ceiling
    floats
A slowly chanted melody of melancholy notes :

> "What tho' the loved form lieth
>   'Neath the dark and dismal sod,
> We know the spirit flieth
>   To the bosom of its God :

> " What tho' our bodies perish—
>   Earth to earth, and dust to dust !
> Are there not hopes to cherish—
>   Fondest hopes in which to trust ?

> " Mourn not the dear departed,
>   For in Death there is no sting !
> Look up, ye broken-hearted !
>   Lo ! the Cross, to which we cling !

> "What tho' the loved form lieth
>   In the Grave's polluting breath,
> We know the Soul defieth
>   All that thou canst do, oh, Death ! "

Sepulchral Psalms and Choral chants have ceased
    their sounds o'erhead,

The surpliced Priest hath read the solemn Ritual of
    the Dead,
Now friendly mourners slowly step behind that sable
    bier,
Whilst Evelyn, by her father's side, conceals the fall-
    ing tear ;
And Leonardo, too, hath wept o'er Lucia's dusky
    pall,
And shrinks to hear the cold, dank clods upon her
    coffin fall ;
The silent grave hath o'er her closed.   She sleeps,
    Death's pale, pale bride—
As sweet a flower as e'er hath bloomed, or e'er in
    June hath died.

II.

The long, soft Summer days have come and gone,
And Evelyn's fair young face, no longer wan
And wet with grief, its wonted color wears,
And oft she smiles, as erst in earlier years.
Within the sound of Arno's dashing foam,
Where the rough waters of the river roam
Around the base of rugged Appenine,
'Twixt banks of jasmine and the eglantine,
A Tuscan villa rears its sunlit dome—

'Tis Leonardo Vecchi's summer home.
Within its walls hath Evelyn's father found
Relief from care, and oft those halls resound
With Albert's Chorus, mingling with the strains
Of Evelyn's music, as the evening wanes ;
And, sometimes, when the air is softly calm,
This youthful pair is rambling in the balm
Of eventide, to watch the eddying flow
Of Arno wandering on its way below,
Or, slowly strolling thro' some sylvan vale,
When fire-flies twinkle in the twilight's pale,
They list the warblings of the nightingale.

'Twas thus the Summer and the Autumn past,
And Winter with its rude Trans-Alpine blast,
Around "fair Florence" too benign to roar,
Grows milder as he nears the Tuscan shore.
And, now, in orange groves the orioles sing
Their grateful pæans to returning Spring ;
Around the oak more closely clings the vine,
And tender hearts more closely yet entwine ;
Whilst blossoms catch the kisses of the dew,
And maidens meditate, and lovers woo.
'Tis twilight's quickening time—the trysting hour
Of Orient climes, when trembling leaf and flower

Are shimmering in the starlight's silver sheen,
And silence softens all the sleeping scene.

   Against the Gothic gate, she holds ajar,
Sweet Evelyn leans, more brilliant than the star
Her eyes have sought. With crimson•lips apart,
Her life-blood bounding thro' her heart,
She lists to wooing words, which welcome steal
Within her soul—Affection's first appeal.

   What wonder is there Albert should adore
This young and lovely girl—that he should pour
His wealth of love on one so good and fair,
And warmly breathe it in her willing ear?

   Like faint-remembered parts of some soft dream,
Young Albert's fervent tones to Evelyn seem;
As some sweet thought, the more 'tis pondered
    o'er,
The mind admits as once conceived before,
So dormant love, within her spirit stirred,
Enkindles newly with each whispered word.
These vows and burning words, in Evelyn's breast,
Have warmed to flame a fervor unconfest—
Love's latent sparks—its half-extinguished gleams
Her heart hath harbored but in flitting dreams;
And yet, alas! these throbbings must be hushed—
Her love, requited—by denial crushed!

The fiat of a father's iron will
Hath quivered in her soul with sudden thrill;
Before her Memory stands, Iconoclast,
A startling spectre of the buried Past—
That hand betrothed ere e'en to girlhood grown,
That hand, by Albert asked, is not her own—
'Tis this she murmurs in her lover's ear—
By kind unkindness dooms him to despair.
  With sinking heart, another's promised bride,
Hath sorrowing Evelyn shrunk from Albert's side.
O'er Evelyn's tingling cheek and Albert's woe,
Come Night, kind Night, thy veiling vesture throw.

  Time's deep discordant tones from yonder tower
Hath tolled the midnight's melancholy hour;
The rolling river, with its ceaseless moan,
Makes lone, sad hearts feel sadder and more lone,
Whilst Evelyn struggles with a vain regret,
Her sleepless pillow with her weeping wet.
And other eyes there are, which cannot sleep—
Aye, other eyes that would, but cannot weep:
Whole years of thought, of sober, solemn thought,
And high resolves that teeming brain hath wrought
Thro' that long night, and ere the early dawn
A rider leaves the gate.   'Tis Albert gone!

Gone, ay, gone—but he knows not, cares not where!
Ay, gone for many a lone and weary year!
Gone from the mellow meads and Tuscan vales!
Gone from the soft songs of the nightingales!
Gone from the citron-groves, where, side by side,
He walked with his love in the eventide!
Gone, with a load of grief upon his breast!
Anywhere, anywhere to find him rest!

'Tis night—an Indian-summer's softest night—
  'Tis late, and the great city seems to sleep;
  The pale stars only their long vigils keep,
Mellowing harsh angles with their silver light;
The City rests—and motionless lies all,
  Save in one quarter, thro' the lighted doors
And curtained windows of a princely hall
  A flood of merriment and music pours.
Within is Northern Fashion's rich display,
  For Philadelphia's fairest of her fair.
Her wealth and pride, her gallant and her gay,
  With sober age and jocund youth are there.
The hours to gladness and the dance belong,
To wine and wit, to sentiment and song;
Here Matrons prim with gray-haired Sires converse,
There moneyed Merchants talk of Stock and Burse:

2

Now Prudence shocked, is whispering of the faults
Of belles less modest, whirling in the waltz,
Whilst timid girlhood, with its furtive glance,
Regards the bashful boy who claims the dance.

But follow we that form in spotless white—
Yon flitting form, so fairy-like and light—
See! how she walks the newly waxen floor,
As now she passes thro' the spacious door!
Beyond the bustling ball-room's fitful glare,
To breathe the moisture of the morning air,
With memory busy at her bosom's core,
She seeks the quiet of the corridor.

Alas! the heavy heart may wear, awhile,
Before the careless world, its gayest smile,
And mirth may sparkle in the tear-wet eye,
Like sunshine thro' September's hazy sky,
But soon that clouded heart, surcharged with grief,
Must wildly break, or weeping, find relief!

That fair, familiar face is once more wan,
That winning smile she lately wore is gone;
Her tapering fingers to her young heart prest,
The starlight stealing o'er her snow-white breast,
Her pale, pale lips apart, she breathes a prayer,
Whilst in her eye there sits a trembling tear.
But scarce upon her lips her prayer hath died,

When stealing, like a spectre, to her side,
That kinsman, whom her inmost spirit loathed—
Her slighted suitor, scorned—her feared betrothed,
Whom from her shrinking **side,** erst-while she
    spurned—
Her evil genius hath again **returned,**
And, there, beneath the **dusky** night's **noon-tide**
Hath clasped and claimed her as his promised bride.
    "Ah, yes!" he whispers low, with flushing brow,
"Ah, yes! proud Evelyn, you may scorn **me now,**
But, **by** your father's pledged and **solemn** vow,
By every word these lips have ever spoke,
By Andrew Hunter's **oath,** which **ne'er was broke,**
And by **our kindred blood, I tell thee here,**
Come weal, or woe, by foul means, or by fair,
That, **spurn me as you will, this** hand of thine—
That heart—thy haughty self shall yet be mine."
    His grasp is loosed; then speaks her woman's heart:
" Now hear me, Andrew Hunter, ere we part!
By Him who rules our hearts—our God above—
By Him, who knits together hearts in love,
By that unseen—that lythe, mysterious chain,
By which are linked in one **the wedded twain,**
By all the virtues which **the soul adorn,**
I tell thee, sir, **this** breast recoils **with scorn**

From hollow nuptial vows, unblest above—
From empty oaths that give the lie to love."

The restless wheels of Time are rolling on,
Year after year on sombre wing hath gone ;
Again Glen Arvon's garnished walls repeat
The sound of Evelyn's lightly falling feet.
Sole mistress of that cottage she presides,
By all beloved, and oft she gently guides
Her aged father to his cushioned chair,
Then steals away to hide the anxious tear,
That will unbidden start from eyes, as sweet
As e'er a father's fondest gaze did meet.
And sometimes, too, those love-lit eyes are dim
With tears ; and yet those tears are not for him,
But nightly, as she lowly kneels to pray,
She weeps and prays for one who 's far away—
Aye, far away, alas ! she knows not where—
She only feels, to her how deeply dear
(Neath Arctic skies, or Bengal's burning sun,)
Is now the welfare of that absent one.
And ofttimes, too, he is flitting thro' her dreams,
As once he was, or else he lifeless seems,
A lonely corse, with glazed and ghastly eye
Forever gazing on the glaring sky.

And, thus, passed Evelyn's girlhood sadly by.
Meanwhile, those fearful years are drawing nigh,
Which soon must shake her country from its base,
And sweep, like Simoom, o'er her haughty race.
E'en now, those wrathful clouds are lowering nigh,
Which, tinged with blood, bedim the Nation's sky—
E'en now, the muttering of the storm is heard—
From realm to realm the peaceful land is stirred,
Whilst Freedom, turning pale with sad affright,
Hath plumed her wings prelusive to her flight!
 That noble fabric by our fathers reared,
By blood cemented, and by all revered,
Alas! is tottering now, for Discord there
Hath dwelt, with angry look, for many a year;
See Tyrant-rule, defiant of the Right,
Hath throned itself despotic in its might,
And sends its minions thro' the startled land
In mad career, with naked steel in hand,
Till Justice, yielding all that she can yield,
Hath drawn her Sword, and bears aloft her Shield!

III.

The moon looks down on Eutaw's classic plain,
Where sleep the ashes of the silent slain,
Where fourscore years of winter-winds and rains

Have scarce effaced the conflict's crimson stains.
Beside the sunken graves of hero-sires
Unflinching sons have lit their signal fires,
Which call the young and old from home and
    hearth,
And check the maidens in their Christmas mirth,
Whilst weeping wives lament their parting ones,
And mothers mourn o'er battle-summoned sons.
'Tis Carolina calls—they cannot pause—
Their lots are linked in one great common cause;
To Carolina right—or Carolina wrong—
Their lives, their fortunes and themselves belong:
Few words they speak; in councils bold, but brief,
They gather round their gallant, chosen chief;
Beneath yon flag, that flaps the frosty air,
'Tis Albert Ashleigh's voice breaks silence there:

    "Sons of the South," he cries, "awake!
      To arms! 'Tis your Country's call!
    She bids you battle for her sake,
      Or with her Freedom fall:
    Forth to the field go meet the foe,
    Defend her with your best blood's flow:
    To arms! Give blow for blow
        In Freedom's Cause!

"Sons of the injured South, arise!
   To your native land's release!
Be deaf to cries of 'Compromise'—
   To coward calls for 'Peace:'
. *Now* is the day: no longer **wait**,
She bids you *now* decide her fate;
Arm! ere it be too late,
                    In Freedom's Cause!

" Men of the South! what **wait** ye for?
   Your enemy is in the field;
'Irrepressible' is the war—
   Ye must not—cannot yield:
Must Southern men their wrongs be taught?
Can men, born free, so base be brought?
Fight—as your fathers fought
                    In Freedom's Cause!

" Lo! the proud flash of Beauty's eye
   Trusts her Country to your care!
She bids you to the battle hie;
   Go with her holy prayer:
On! while a hostile soul survives!
On! for your sisters and your wives!
Your Honor and your lives
                    In Freedom's Cause!

"The Lord of Justice knows your wrongs,
  .   He will be your Strength and Shield;
To craven slaves alone belongs
     The spirit that could yield:
Think of your Country's honored dead—
Marion's brave men o'er Eutaw led—
Remember how they bled
           In Freedom's Cause!

" Men of the suffering South, arise!
     There is a victory to be won:
The glorious work before you lies:
     The battle is begun:
Up with the Red-cross!   On, ye brave!
Let its proud folds in triumph wave,
Or—'neath it find a grave
           In Freedom's Cause!

"To arms! to arms! your Country save:
       On God rely:
       Your foe defy:
Fixed on the Red-cross every eye—
       Oh! let it wave
       O'er spirits brave,
Resolved to do—or die
           In Freedom's Cause!"

Thus Albert speaks. A hundred youthful braves,
Above whose heads "the Red-cross" banner waves,
Beside him kneel on Eutaw's classic sod,
And there commit their Country's Cause to God—
Beneath the stars of that cold Christmas sky
They swear in Freedom's Cause to do—or die.

Ah! many a tear, that widowed hearts have wept,
Attests how well that faithful vow is kept:
From solemn Sumter's sea-girt, shaken rock,
To desperate Antietam's shivering shock.
On many a bloody charge, by Albert led,
On many a gory field they leave their dead,
Till few of all this Patriot-band remain—
The living few that mourn the many slain.

Again 'tis night—a moonless, black December
    night ;
Strange sounds are heard from Stafford's cannon-
    crested height—
Mysterious sounds, commingling with the murmur-
    ing flow
Of Rappahannock rushing o'er its rocks below :
All night the whispered bidding, and the muffled oar,
Have reached the ear on Spottsylvania's guarded
    shore,

3

Where lie those veteran "Leesburg-heroes," undis-
    mayed—
The iron-hearted Barksdale, and his brave Brigade.
  Three times, their stubborn foes have sought the
    Southern bluff,
Three times their bridge of boats has spanned the
    waters rough,
Before the Mississippians' deadly rifle fire,
Three times, their reeling ranks with bleeding steps
    retire :
Full fifteen hours, with crashing shot and shrieking
    shell,
They storm the cliff—at length, with one loud, thrill-
    ing yell,
Those cruel hordes have crossed the troubled stream,
And o'er the quaking hills their bristling bayonets
    gleam.
Now all the vales are torn by galling cannonade,
God help that small, heroic band—that bold brigade—
Which will not turn and flee, but, foot by foot, disputes
The City's ancient soil, which savage foe pollutes,
Till night hath gathered o'er that City's toppling
    spires,
That Ghoul-like gleam before the foemen's flickering
    fires.

The long night wanes. The picket, on his silent post,
Keeps cautious, constant watch o'er Burnside's slum-
     bering host :
Sleep on—for ere to-morrow's evening stars will rise,
Full many a one, in Death's cold sleep, will close his
     eyes !

Long rolls the loud Reveille-drum. The Army
     wakes.
O'er Fred'ricksburg's now warlike streets the morn-
     ing breaks,
Whilst 'gainst the sky "the Southern Cross" is seen
     to shine—
'Tis lion-hearted Lee in long-drawn battle line.
Lo! war-worn Longstreet's veteran Corps, in grim
     array,
In moody, anxious silence, waiting for the fray !
See, yonder comes the young, but wondrous can-
     noneer—
Prompt Pelham, glancing o'er his guns with prudent
     care !
And Stuart, too, the dauntless, dashing cavalier,
The Knightly son of Scotland's kingly line, is there ;
His Falcon-eye hath spied fierce Sumner's chosen
     corps,

In double-quick-time, charging 'cross the hazy moor:
Then rings that clarion voice: "Up! Gunners, to
    your posts!
Aim well, my gallant men! Hurl back the hireling
    hosts!"
One mingled burst of smoke: one long, low-rumbling
    sound—
War's iron messengers, with ricochetting bound,
Have smote the staggered foe, and in one common
    mound,
The dying and the dead bestrew the frozen ground.
A moment—and their rallying ranks have closed
    again:
With grim, defiant shout they shake the trembling
    plain:
A hundred answering cannon, in their ruthless ire,
O'er hill and glade are belching forth their vengeful
    fire.

But who is he, that furious, frenzied foe must front—
Whose bulwark-breast must bravely bear the battle's
    brunt?
Behold him there with lofty look, almost divine,
Fleet as the Lightning, lead his Legions into line!
As sweeps the swift Sirocco o'er the Syrian main,

And leaves within its track a wrecked and ruined
    train:
Now here, now there—with thunder-force—above,
    below,
He hurls his conquering columns 'gainst the charging
    foe:
Ah! woe betide the rash assailants that essay
To cope, on battle-field, with Jackson's giant-sway—
Resistless Jackson—besom of the bloody fray!

  Meantime, not all the numbers of those Northern
    hordes—
Not all the pristine prowess of their Country's swords
Can storm that wall before Marye's embattled height,
Where Kershaw and McLaws unflinching face the
    fight:
Lo! trooping o'er the dale, in dashing, martial style,
See Meagher's stalwart men of Erin's distant isle!—
Fierce scions of that fiery race, which won at Waterloo
And Fontenoy's field of blood, come bursting into
    view!

    Their starry banners waved on high,
    Their bayonets gleaming 'gainst the sky,
    The Armies of the South defy—
        Her chosen chivalry:

Forward they come
With 'larum drum,
Thro' sun and shade,
Neath cannonade
    And musketry!

The smoke, in columns, laps the plain,
The din, that swells above the main,
Is echoed o'er the hills again
    In dreadful harmony!
        Neath shot and shell,
        With shout and yell,
        They cross the glade
        And esplanade,
            Aye, gallantly!

On! on! they come!—too late to pause—
They dash against the grim McLaws,
Onward, into the very jaws
    Of Death, undauntedly!
        Their muskets flash!
        Their bayonets clash!
        O'er mangled dead
        The living tread
            Unsteadily!

As when rough billows, breaking o'er
The reefs of Hatteras' boisterous shore,
Are ebbing to the sea once more,
    Receding rapidly,
      So backward borne,
      With banners torn,
      Athwart the glen
      These maddened men
        Press franticly!

Now sinks the blood-red setting sun ;
Hushed is the hot, yet smoking gun ;
The strife is o'er ; the South has won
    That dear-bought victory.
      That gory field
      The foemen yield—
      Their bravest quail,
      Whilst pennons trail
        Despairingly!

The blushing moon is peering thro' the clouds
    o'erhead,
Illuming all the grisly field of ghastly dead :
In doleful requiem, the night-winds' fitful moans,
Anon, are mingling with the parting Spirits' groans.

See! o'er yon well-known form a group of soldiers
    sob!

'Tis Longstreet's martial chieftain—Georgia's gallant
    Cobb!

Sleep on, thou martyred hero! in thy glory sleep!

Long o'er thy gory grave shall Georgia's children weep,

And, grateful for thy many deeds, the memory keep

Of Cobb and Victory. And, there! behold a bleed-
    ing one!

That "grand old Roman," Gregg, his Country's
    noblest son,

Who fought for Freedom's sake, and scorned the
    world's applause,

The first to draw his sword in suffering Freedom's
    Cause:

His lips, tho' pale and parched, with life-blood ebbing
    low,

Are whispering words of cheer, in accents faint and
    slow—

" Let Carolinians know how cheerfully I die,

Contending for their Rights—their Homes — and
    Liberty."

  Lo! all but lifeless lies, on yonder litter borne,

A loved, but humbler one, whom faithful comrades
    mourn;

With tearful eyes and swelling breasts they bear him on
O'er field and tangled fen, and up the open lawn,
Within Glen Arvon's friendly door, where tender hands
Await to welcome weary ones.　　There Evelyn stands!
They lay him at her feet, their blankets o'er him
　　spread,
They leave him lying there, his knapsack 'neath his
　　head :
That form they followed oft along the marches' toil,
Which led them o'er Manassas' twice victorious soil ;
That cheering voice, which bade them "Charge" at
　　Malvern Hill—
That form seems scarcely breathing now—that voice
　　is still :
His brave young breast, so cruel torn by foeman's shot,
Still true to Evelyn beats; yet Evelyn knows him not,
But, patient, lingers there, to watch his wavering
　　pulse,
Whilst pangs of racking pain his fevered frame con-
　　vulse.

　The anxious night hath passed, whilst Evelyn's
　　careful hands
Have smoothed the choicest couch her father's cot
　　commands.

The Winter's sun creeps slowly up the vaulted skies:
But once has Albert Ashleigh oped his languid eyes,
And gazing into Evelyn's face with sweet surprise,
Half-dreaming, faintly breathes her name.   Yet, still
    he sleeps,
Whilst Evelyn o'er his couch her faithful vigil keeps:
She sighs in secret grief: she soothes his fevered brow,
Then smiles between her tears—*because she knows him*
    now!

Oh! ye, who in the midst of Battle's fiercest storms,
Have, weary, watched and prayed o'er loved and
    bleeding forms—
Ye weeping, widowed Rachels, whose heroic worth,
In secret, brightly shone beside the lonely hearth,
Who've felt War's whelming waters o'er you coldly
    roll—
Ye know what waves of anguish surged o'er Evelyn's
    soul!

IV.

The Winter has vanished: the roses of Spring
    Are kissed by the Sun of the second of May;
The birds in the woodlands bewitchingly sing
    To hearts, at Glen Arvon, that are happy to-day.

The daffodils bend 'neath the dew of the dawn,
   And pink-eyed anemones enamel the way,
Whilst tiny, pale daisies look up from the lawn
   At Evelyn and Albert, who are walking to-day.

Adown the gray rocks the rills ripple and bound
   Far over the meadows in rythm and play,
With many a mystical, musical sound,
   To welcome the loved and the loving to-day.

Yon roguish young Robin, in flashing red vest,
   His throat all aglow with the joy of his lay,
Is chirping and chatting to his mate, in her nest,
   Of some one he knows, who is wooing to-day.

The Lark is aloft!   See, how swiftly she flies!
   But why is her song so enchantingly gay?
She laves her light wing in the blue of the skies,
   And warbles of one who is happy to-day.

Adown the arched West sink the beams of the Sun,
   Serenely the moments are passing away;
Two hearts, at the Cottage, are beating as one—
   Two hearts, at Glen Arvon, are happy to-day.

   The evening wanes.   Before Glen Arvon's gate
There halts a Courier, who hath ridden late,

And hurried, leaves a note in Albert's hand—
A hasty summons to his new command.

No time for words: with one warm, fond adieu,
Hath Albert crossed the fields from Evelyn's view,
Nor turns, nor reins his onward, quick career,
Till warlike sounds have smote his soldier-ear.

Once more, before Marye's embattled height
Three thousand score of men, at dead of night,
In gloomy line, in battle's grim array,
Are anxious watching for the coming day.

Just as the first red streaks of early dawn
Have lit with life the Sabbath's sacred morn,
The foe, in phalanx firm, is scaling fast
Marye's rough ramparts to the trumpet's blast.
There Barksdale and his gallant band, again,
Must meet the shock of twenty thousand men:
They fight, as never heroes fought before;
They fight till running rills of human gore
Have drenched the hills, yet still they stubborn stand
Before the foe, with muskets clubbed in hand.
Then 'gainst them Sedgwick bursts—his columns
    massed—
With force of Avalanche, his hordes, at last,
On right and left, have turned their feeble flanks,
And backward bear their brave, unbroken ranks:

Still Barksdale bays his foe ; he will not flinch,
But, fighting, yields the field, now inch by inch.

Oh ! for the daring dash of Jackson now !
But woeful Sabbath morn ! O'er Jackson's brow,
Alas ! the dews of death are gathering fast,
Whilst all the Nation, wailing, stands aghast !

Behold ! meanwhile from Sedgwick's shouting corps
A rampant rabble sweeping cross the moor !
O'er field, o'er fence they bound; thro' brake and brush,
In reckless, wild career they onward rush,
And trampling o'er Glen Arvon's peaceful grounds,
They fiercely yell, till all the vale resounds.
　But lo ! the leader of that lawless crew—
Yon form, which shames the shameful Northern blue—
Stained Livery of Oppression's retinue !
Does trembling Evelyn mark that ruffian face—
The ruthless robber of her ruined race ?
Too well, alas ! that gloating eye she knows—
Most dreaded of her Country's dastard foes !
Alas ! that Andrew Hunter's traitor hand
Should wield his sword against his mother-land !
　Behold him rudely pushing thro' that door,
Which oft has kindly welcomed him of yore !

He strides across the Hall to Evelyn's side,
And hails her roughly as his " Rebel Bride."
Quoth he: "Come, Evelyn, come—my love—my life—
My pretty prisoner now—ere long, my wife."

" *Thy* wife! Sir!" Evelyn cries, " I own with shame,
That Andrew Hunter bears my noble name;
I blush, that kindred drops course thro' our veins:
These tingling checks confess that Treason stains
The bright Escutcheon of our honored race,
But 'tis *thy* deeds have doomed it to Disgrace:
Call *me* not 'wife.' With all thy subtlest hate
Strike at this heart! I'd bless thee for my fate,
Ere I would wed thee—traitor to thy State!"

"Preach not to me," he tauntingly replies,
"More specious are thy Rebel creeds than wise:
Go call thy father, girl! for him I seek."

" There comes my father! sir, but far too weak
To bear the cruel words, methinks, thou'lt speak."

"Well, sir! how fares it with mine Uncle now?
It seems since last I saw that *loyal* brow,
Full many a trace of care hath o'er it crossed,
And War's rough years have added to the frost
Of Winter on those locks. But come! 'tis late!
To business now: yon Chaplain at the gate,
And these, my soldiers here, my bidding wait."

"Thy business, sir?" the old man asks, "Speak on:
What tho' thou be my loved, dead Sister's son,
I hate the deeds thy father's race hath done!
Ye, one and all—our brethren but in name—
From Pulpit and from Press our land defame;
With foul-tongued clamor and maligning mouth,
Ye carp and cavil at the hated South:
Ye prate of peace, and yet, in savage ire
Ye desolate our shores with war and fire—
With chains and swords o'errun our peaceful plains—
Swords for the valiant—for the vanquished, chains!
Your flag so honored once, on land and sea,
So long the symbol of a people free—
That flag, which rallied erst the Nation's braves,
No longer o'er their gallant lineage waves,
But license lends to mercenary knaves,
To bind us 'neath its folds as vanquished slaves,
Or fill our smiling South with bloody graves!
With earnest pride I, too, long, long upheld
That banner once, and oft this heart hath swelled,
Remembering all my perils, and the scars
Received beneath its conquering Stripes and Stars;
But I have marked my Country's wrongs and woe—
Myself have felt each fratricidal blow,
That makes Virginia's rich, best blood to flow,

And ne'er again can call that flag 'my own,'
Which costs my Country one complaining groan."
  That voice is hushed. With anger scarce controlled,
The Northman quick replies: "Thy words are bold—
Too bold for one, whose loud disloyal tongue
Had best be silent; for thou'lt find, ere long,
Thy safety, and thine Evelyn's too, depends
On whom, as foes, thy rebel speech offends."
  "Speak on! What more does Tyranny demand?
Would'st drive me helpless from my house and land?
If blood thou seek'st, thy minions I defy;
Thy Grandsire's son will teach thee how to die."
  "Ye are my prisoners—thou and Evelyn—both:
I claim fulfillment of thy plighted troth—
Thy daughter's hand: renewal of thine oath
Of true allegiance to our Nation's laws,
And firm resistance to this Rebel Cause.
Refuse—and naught will save thee from the doom
Deserved, for yonder torches shall consume
These loved, these venerable ancestral halls,
Till not a stone of all Glen Arvon's walls
Shall one upon another rest—till all
It boasts shall in one common ruin fall."
  "Then hear me, Andrew Hunter!" he replies,
"Thine oath: thy high behests, I all despise:

So bid your heroes to their valiant work—
Fit deed for heart of Vandal or of Turk:
For Tyrant! I would see my daughter dead
By my own act, ere I would have her wed
The traitor hand, to which that sword belongs—
Foul, bloody symbol of her country's wrongs!
Would'st have me swear allegiance to that hand,
Which desolates my unoffending land—
That hand, which e'en its own Virginia smites—
Which, ruthless, robs me of my dearest Rights?
Ye have spoiled me of my own—my all—'tis true!
Thank God! ye cannot touch my Honor too!
Apply your torch!   Bind on oppression's chains!
Thank God! at least, my Honor yet remains!
Virginian born—Virginian I will die,
And meet my doom without one coward sigh!"

 Beneath the dark shades of the gathering gloom,
The flames of Glen Arvon the forests illume!
The flashes of blaze o'er the beeches arise,
The smoke, in black columns, envelopes the skies;
Tall figures of foemen are gliding about,
Like Demons of Darkness, they dance and they shout,
They revel and gloat, in their glee and their hate—
Poor wretches! nor wot they their terrible fate!

 4

A rider hath ridden, all reeking and hot,
Post-haste to Glen Arvon, pursued to the spot :—
"Now quick! to your ranks! to the river!" he
    cries,
"The Rebels are on us; we have suffered surprise;
We are flanked; we are routed at Chancellorsville,
Where Jackson has fallen, but Stuart and Hill,
Revenging his fate, all their cohorts have massed,
And drive us before them as leaves on the blast,
Whilst Sedgwick, defeated, is fast falling back
With Early and Wilcox like wolves on his track!"

His warning comes late: ere its echo hath died,
A troop of stout horsemen up gallantly ride—
Young Ashleigh their leader—as cavalier band
As sabre e'er drew in defence of their land!
Woe! woe! to the foemen, who fearfully flee,
Concealing themselves behind bramble and tree!
As Falcons swoop down on each panic-struck bird!
The Southrons surround them—a cowering herd!
The Captors are Captive! but where is their Chief
Hath wrought on Glen Arvon this ruin and grief?

What warrior so valiant—what soldier so bold
Midst frail, feeble women, the helpless and old,
As he, who, alarmed, slinks away like the deer—
The first to scent danger, when battle is near!

But Albert is weary of Carnage and Death,
And orders his horsemen their sabres to sheath :
"No blood must be spilled! Men, remember!" he
cries,
"For 'Vengeance is Mine, saith the Lord' of the
skies."

Before Glen Arvon's ruined walls there stand
Brave Ashleigh and his Evelyn, hand in hand.
Ah! happy Evelyn, by her father blest,
Her young head sheltered on his aged breast,
Whilst 'neath the startled Midnight's dewy air
A Chaplain weds the Valiant to the Fair!
Weird wedding-lights, those waning midnight stars!
Strange witnesses, those sturdy Sons of Mars!
But Venus waits on bold Minerva's car,
And Love must yield to sterner calls of War!

Off, thro' the shadows of the night's noontide—
Off, 'neath the solemn, sombre trees they ride!
"God shield the Soldier and his long-loved Bride!"
"God bless the old Virginian by their side!"
Off, off they go, with blessings and the prayers
Of gallant Carolina Cavaliers!

V.

Near two and twenty months of anxious hopes and
    fears,
Near two and twenty months of woman's yearning
    tears,
Near two and twenty mournful months have passed
    away,
Since that eventful, oft-remembered night of May;
Whilst, far from fearful scenes of battle and of blood,
Where, close by Eutaw's plain, steals Santee's sullen
    flood,
Beloved of friends, 'mid all that easy comfort gives,
In Albert's Carolina home his Evelyn lives—
Yet *lonely* lives, for sleeping 'neath the stranger's soil
Her father rests, forever freed from war and toil,
And far away, on many a field's ensanguined marge,
Her daring Albert, dauntless, leads the desperate
    charge.

Now, War hath bared anew his blood-red, brawny
    arm ;
Throughout the struggling South is pealed the loud
    alarm !
The Hydra-headed foe looms up from out the West,
And proudly lifts aloft his cruel, crimsoned crest :

His countless hosts rush down o'er Georgia's fated soil,
Her fairest homes destroy ; her Temples all despoil.
  What now avails the prowess of our valiant arms
'Gainst foes, that soon as fallen rise in myriad swarms?
Alas ! our bootless sacrifice of bravest blood !
What arm of flesh can stay the whelming Vandal-
     flood ?
Now hourly sinking in the trembling scale of Fate,
No hand, it seems, can save our shivering Ship of
     State :
Our Country's Starry Cross is seen to wane on high,
And ill-foreboding darkness dims the Southern sky.

  Behold! o'er Carolina's plains the Intruder sweep!
Behind him homesteads smoke! Lo! wretched women
     weep!
Behold the harrowing scenes of torture in his trail!
Hark! starving children cry! Alas! the woeful wail!
  And now he nears the Santee's myrtle-shaded shore;
O'er Eutaw's classic field his merc'less minions pour :
Heaven help poor trembling Evelyn in her lonely
     woe,   .
No manly, loving arm to shield her from the foe !
On, on they come ! Weep, Evelyn, weep in wild
     Despair!

The Wolf his victim seeks: a worse than foe is near;
Thy nest he knows!   Behold! those eyes upon thee
    glare!
Behold the Traitor, Andrew Hunter, standing there!

    Torn from her husband's home by force of fiendish
      foe,
As Andrew Hunter's trembling prize, compelled to go,
Now long and bitterly poor Evelyn weeps. 'Tis vain:
She goes, a guarded Captive, in the Conqueror's train;
Beneath her Kinsman's watchful eye, all woe-begone,
She weeps till night, and thro' the dreary night till
    dawn.
    But, ever on them both another Human Eye,
Tho' never seeming near, hath played the cautious spy;
Familiar with each spot, it marks each path and pass,
And deftly follows on the living, moving mass,
But never Evelyn recks, that Albert's faithful Slave
Against her Captor plots, her wretched self to save.
    Another night is nigh—another night in camp,
And Evelyn, shivering in the evening's piercing damp,
The foemen's fire hath sought—her look of blank
    despair
Gives way to wakened Hope—that honest Slave
    draws near—

One cheering look of homage gives, then, off again,
He seeks the Rebel camp of Hampton's gallant men.

As gazes the Eagle, with riveted eye,
Adown on his prey, from his eyrie on high,
So Hampton, the chiefest of brave Cavaliers,
Well worthy the Chaplet of Fame which he wears,
Now watching the foe from his high bivouac,
Is wrapt in regarding his point of attack.
Around him the night-breezes fitfully sigh;
The cold moon above him is scaling the sky:
The spirit of Marion revives in his soul:
His Country's lost hopes o'er him sombrely roll;
He reads in her strugglings poor Hungary's fate—
In Poland's dark doom—the knell of his State.
  Below him is rolling the dark Edisto,
Beyond which carouses the Cormorant-foe:
The "Bummers" and Stragglers of Sherman's great
    hosts,
Their Bacchanal Sentries asleep on their posts,
The rough and the rude, in rendezvous there,
Pollute the loose trail of the Army's arriere.
  And who so adapted this crew to command,
As renegade Hunter, the Scourge of his land!
Who, drunk with excesses of blood and debauch,

Uneasily tosses, to-night, on his couch,
Whilst Evelyn, poor Captive, lies down on the sod
And tearfully lifts her sweet eyes to her God.

Now Hampton descending—his eye on the foe—
Hath cautiously moved thro' the valley below;
His horsemen abreast on the river's rough slope,
Shall numbers so few with yon enemy cope?
No sinking of hearts at the difficult task—
'Tis Hampton who leads them—'tis all that they ask!
  "My Soldiers!" he tells them, "we pass not to-
    night,
These turbulent waters, the Northmen to fight;
We need but a handful of cavaliers bold,
To rescue a prisoner yon enemies hold:
What tho' the rough flood at your feet swiftly sweeps,
'Tis Innocence calling—a soldier's wife weeps
In yonder vile camp of the dissolute foe—
That Soldier will lead you—my men, will ye go?"
  "Aye, aye, we are ready!" cry all in a breath,
Aye, aye, lead us on!—to her rescue, or—Death!"
  As Albert, with hope beating high in his breast,
Selects from his comrades the bravest and best,
Behold! a rough boat shooting out from the shore!
How stalwart the arm that is bending each oar!

How glowing that face! that dark face of the Slave,
Exerting his strength the frail captive to save!
  Twelve spirits, as buoyant as men on a hunt,
Now restless and reckless, have rushed to the front :
A dozen stout horsemen are swimming the tide ;
They reach the dark bank of the furthermost side,
And thro' the brown woodlands, and over the vale,
They dauntlessly dash, as on wings of the gale ;
The sentries are passed, the guard is o'erpowered,
And Hunter, surprised, from the conflict hath cowered.
  As swift as the glance of an eye—from his seat
Hath Albert alighted—with action as fleet,
He lifts his young wife to his saddle—and then
Behind her he mounts, and is off with his men !
  Now, back to the boat! aye, for wife, and for life !
Now, back to the river!—Unequal the strife
Of hundreds 'gainst twelve! Hark! already the drum
Hath sounded alarm! They are mounted! They
      come!
With speed of the Whirlwind, thro' bramble and brush,
On, on to the river, in hundreds they rush ;
But Albert has reached, with his Evelyn, the boat,
And stout is the arm at the helm as they float
Adown the swift river, 'neath the moon, side by side,
Whilst daringly stem his bold comrades the tide.
  5

Now, down to the banks the pursuers have dashed,
Hark! o'er the rough waters their rifles have flashed!
Cries Hampton: "Make ready! now steady, each
    rank!
And give them a volley on the opposite bank!"
No sooner 'tis ordered, than gallantly done:
Aye, deadly the aim of each Cavalier's gun!
The foemen are startled! *they falter!* THEY FLEE!
The Southrons are Victors! the Captive is free!
   The smoke clears away: 'neath the moon's silver
    sheen
Three riderless steeds in the rapids are seen—
Their riders—pale corses 'neath the current careen!
But hark! o'er the waters that shrill, piercing shriek,
That curdles the life-blood, and blanches each cheek!
A Woman's wild cry hath gone out on the air;
Her spirit is crushed! 'Tis the wail of Despair!
The boat—aye! the boat hath reached safely the shore,
But Albert within it lies covered with gore!

   Weep! Evelyn, aye, weep! To his fond, faithful
    breast
No more shall thy loved form be tenderly prest:
Thine Albert is dead! By his soldierly arm
No more shall thy Country be shielded from harm:

His voyage down Life's fitful River is o'er,
He reaches the Realms of the Limitless Shore:
His Spirit hath gone on the breath of the breeze,
To rest 'neath the shade of the Heavenly Trees.

    Rests the warrior from his labor,
    Sheathed beside him, rusts his sabre,
    Where the aspens pale and quiver
    By the margin of the river—
        By the banks of Edisto.
    But, thro' blissful, bright Dominions,
    Soars his Soul on spotless pinions,
    Far above the Shining River,
    Waiting to be joined forever
        To that Soul it loved below.

    In a Mad-house doleful, dreary,
    Evelyn wanders woeful, weary;
    In a Mad-house, lowly lying,
    In a Mad-house, slowly dying—
        Slowly dying of Despair:
    With her soul forever saddened,
    All her reason rambling, maddened:
    Every night, a night of Sorrow,
    Hoping for the hopeless morrow
        Of a Mad-house, dark and drear!

Behold! ye canting Saints of Cromwell's Creed!
Fanatic Sons of Puritanic Seed!
Oh! righteous Race of holy Plymouth Rock—
New England's puling, sanctimonious Stock!
Behold! the deeds your sacred tenets taught!
Come view the Wreck your pious hands have wrought!
  As Eden erst in quiet beauty smiled,
Till Satan's trail its flowery banks defiled,
So peaceful passed our happy, halcyon hours,
Till loathsome, crawling 'mongst our sunny flowers,
Ye hissed your venom o'er this land of ours:
Oh! ye who, in the name of Christ and Kirk,
Beneath your robes conceal the Dirk,
Behold the Picture!   'Tis your bloody work!

THE DEATH OF THE MAIDEN.

Thro' a forest sere and sober,
In the golden-clad October,
Autumn-winds were softly sighing,
Summer leaflets falling, flying,
    Lying, dying everywhere!
We were wandering, slowly walking;
I was wooing, lowly talking
(Ah! it seems so very lately!)
With a maiden tall and stately—
    With a maiden frail and fair.

How she lingered whilst she listened,
And her eyes with tear-drops glistened!
All her brow and bosom blushing,
Came her words so gently gushing:
    "Take me—love me—I am thine!"
Ah! those words were whispered lowly,
And that vow, it seemed so holy,
As a Vesper-psalm so saintly,
Falling sweetly, falling faintly,
    As a Psalmody divine!

Sweet those moments of our meeting,
Sweet, tho' few and far too fleeting ;
Halcyon hours of golden dreaming—
All of life with beauty teeming
 In those glorious, golden hours !
Blissful were the thoughts we pondered,
Peaceful all the ways we wandered,
Thro' the woods and meadows mellow,
Thro' the waving fields of yellow,
 Thro' the sunny Autumn flowers.

Came then sickness ; and in anguish
Day by day, we watched her languish,
Watched her waning, watched her wasting,
Oh ! the agony of tasting
 Those mad moments of despair !
Vain were all the arts of healing,
Blight was o'er her beauty stealing ;
Vain my wailing, vain my weeping,
Cruel Death came creeping, creeping,
 Caring not that she was fair.

After one long night of sorrow,
Ere the dawning of the morrow,
From the tapers dimly burning,

Softly to the maiden turning,
    Mourners whispered: "She is dead!"
Doubting, fearing, still uncertain,
Dreading yet to lift the curtain,
Something seemed to hover 'round **her**;
Angels, then, I knew had found her,
    Knew I then her soul had fled.

From her lifeless form they tore me,
From her cold embrace they bore me,
But *our Souls* they could not sever;
We shall meet again forever,
    Ay, forever, hand in hand!
Time is flowing! Time is flowing!
On her grave the grass is growing,
Waves the willow o'er her, weeping,
But her sainted Soul is sleeping,
    Waiting in the Spirit-land.

TO A LEAF ON A LADY'S BREAST.

Ah! little Leaf, how covet I
  Your comfortable rest!
How cosily you seem to lie
  Upon my Lady's breast!
And tho' I know 'twere vain to sigh,
  To be, like thee, caressed;
Yet, oh! how happy I could die
  To be so blessed!

I would I were her favorite flower,
  Nor sunned by Summer sky,
But growing in her chosen bower,
  Beneath her azure eye:
How eagerly I'd lift my head
  To catch her maiden kiss;
Perchance she'd make her breast *my* bed,
  A bed of bliss!

Now nestling on her neck, the while
  I'd list to thoughts within,
Then basking in her sunny smile,
  I'd touch her dimpled chin:

From damask cheek and ruby lip
　　I'd steal a roseate hue ;
Her eyes, my skies, from them I'd sip
　　My only dew.

What tho' I perish 'mid my bliss,
　　So I but hear her sigh !
What pleasure half so sweet as this—
　　Upon her breast to die!
Her warm young bosom be my bier ;
　　My dirge, her lulling breath,
Impassioned still, I'd wanton there—
　　Ay, e'en in death!

LEE'S WELCOME TO COLUMBIA.
(*March 30th*, 1870.)

All day the murky clouds hung low
　　Above the silent City ;
The skies seemed draped in robes of woe—
　　To weep in very pity—
In pity for our wounded pride,
　　In pity for our people,
While, since the dawn, the winds had sighed
　　Round crumbling tower and steeple.

The wrecks of old ancestral halls,
   In all their desolateness,
The ruined walks, and blackened walls
   To Vandal hate bore witness.
Against the sky, the toppling stacks,
   In solemn, sad sedateness,
Seemed sentries on their beaten tracks—
   Grim ghosts of former greatness.

Each sombre mart deserted seemed,
   The day wore dull and dreary,
While men moved on, as men that dreamed,
   With footsteps flagging weary.
But, hark!—that sudden clamor hear!—
   That hum of human voices!
Whilst, everywhere, with shout and cheer,
   The very air rejoices!

One little word, first faintly heard,
   Now thousands echo loudly,
And every Southern heart is stirred,
   And every head held proudly!
Maimed men and matrons shout—"'Tis LEE!"
   Fair maidens swell the chorus;
The children clap their hands in glee;
   The sky grows brighter o'er us.

'Tis he!—'tis he!—the hero, LEE!
  No tyrant sword can sever
Our hearts from him, for he shall be
  The sovereign of them ever.
The tidings leap from street to street,
  Each tongue that name repeating,
And many meet with hastening feet
  To give the hero greeting.

See how the brave old chieftain comes—
  No banners o'er him soaring!
No roll is heard of mighty drums,
  No cannons 'round him roaring.
On every heart himself engraved—
  What need of laurelled arches!
'Neath lifted hats and kerchiefs waved
  Our gray-haired warrior marches.

When, in the Christian cause of Peace,
  His sword was sheathed forever,
With him we wept, that we must cease
  Our brave but vain endeavor:
And still we love him as of old,
  When, 'mongst the dead and dying,
He rode, the boldest of the bold,
  Our foe before him flying.

Ah! 'twas a splendid sight to see
  Our Southern chiefs assembled
To greet their grand old leader, LEE,
  'Fore whom once tyrants trembled!
We are not free, alas!—but we
  Forget our heroes never:
We can but shout: "Long live our LEE!"—
  "The SOUTH and LEE forever!"

WHAT THE ANGEL BROUGHT US.

In the early days of Autumn,
  In the bright Autumnal days,
When the Indian-summer sunlight
  Slants its soft September rays;
In my chamber I lay dreaming
  Of a sick one dear to me—
Of her young maternal yearnings
  For a Life, that was to be.

By her bed-side I was dreaming
  In the curtained light of day,
Till the purpling of the morning
  Brightened into streaks of gray—

I was dreaming that an Angel,
  Hovering o'er the loved one's couch,
Fanned her with a breath of Heaven—
  Healed her with his holy touch;

Seeming, too, to carry something—
  Something sheltered 'neath his wing:
Then he laid it down and left it—
  Left the wee, but wondrous thing.
And he scarcely pressed the carpet,
  Passing by me, where I lay—
Touched me with his wing as lightly
  As an Aspen leaf at play.

Yet, that gentle touch awoke me,
  And the rosy flush of dawn,
Falling on the lovely sufferer,
  Showed the Angel-form was gone;
But I saw the Angel's burden
  Tightly to her bosom pressed—
Baby fingers, as she slumbered,
  Toying with her marble breast.

And I kissed the dainty fingers,
  While two lips so sweetly smiled,

Could I tell which was the sweetest—
    Mother pale or dimpled child?
But I know, no Angel ever
    Sweeter boon or blessing bore;
And no Father and no Mother
    Welcomed such a Babe before.

For her face is like the morning,
    Like the morning-star her eye,
And her hair is like the sunlight
    Of the Indian-summer sky.
Such the gift the Angel brought us—
    Baby with her winsome ways,
In the early days of Autumn,
    In the bright Autumnal days.

MAD.

The pale-faced Moon in a fleecy cloud
   Lies cold and blank in her curtained bed,
Like a visage veiled in a snowy shroud—
   The stark, stiff face of a woman dead.
Avaunt, pale vision!   Out, out from the sky!
   I know whose face is reflected there—
That woman's face, with its dead, dull eye,
   That chills my veins with its vacant stare.

Just so she looked, when they laid her down
   With marks of blood on her face and feet;
With tell-tale stains on her tattered gown,
   Just so she lay in her winding sheet:
Just so she seemed in a cloud to float,
   While my senses reeled and my sight grew dim
With murder marks on her pearly throat,
   Just so she paled as a spectre grim.

'Twas years ago, on a shadowy night,
   One Christmas-eve of the long ago,
The moon looked down with a lurid light
   On the wild and wintry world below—

With baleful beams, through a boughless glade,
  Peered mournfully down at Maud and me,
As we silent paused in the solemn shade,
  In the fitful shade of a sombre tree.

The night seemed weird, as the dead leaves stirred
  Over our heads in the hoary tree,
Whilst never a word, not a whispered word
  Was spoken at all by Maud or me:
For my brain was crazed by the Demon, Wine,
  My body was reeling to and fro,
While the moon turned pale, ashamed to shine
  On the sorrowful scene of sin below.

As we stood in silence, side by side,
  In the dismal shade of the dusky tree,
In the gloomy haze of the night's noon-tide,
  How beautiful seemed my Maud to me!
But the damning Bowl my brain had crazed,
  My blood beat fast with its subtle flow,
And the moon alone saw my arm upraised,
  Only the moon saw the fatal blow.

    *   *   *   *   *   *

How gracefully lay my Maud at rest,
  Her beautiful raven hair afloat,

With gems of blood on her jewelled breast,
  With beads of blood on her pearly throat!
Ah! I loved my lovely Maud that night,
  As the moon fell full on her upturned face,
And wanton winds, o'er her bosom white,
  Were lightly lifting the envied lace!

We slept—both slept till the Christmas-dawn,
  Dreaming our dreams till the break of day;
I dreamed that my beautiful Maud was gone,
  Gone with the beams of the moon away.
I woke—and my hands were fast in chains,
  And felon fetters were around my feet,
Whilst Maud, all marred with murder stains,
  Lay stark and stiff in a winding sheet.

I watched my Maud in her flowing shroud,
  I watched till my weeping eyes were dim,
Till she seemed to float on a fleecy cloud,
  Paling away as a spectre grim:
And I see her yet beyond the stars,
  I watch her form in the midnight sky,
I see her face through my prison bars—
  That woman's face with its dead, dull eye.

G

They call me mad, and with felon chains
   They bind me fast to my prison floor,
Where I nightly hear the mournful strains
   Of the winter winds in their wild uproar;
Where naught I hear but my clanking chains
   And the howling winds at my dungeon door,
Where naught I see but the mocking stains
   Of that face in the moon forever-more.

Avaunt, pale moon, with your ghostly glare!
·   Look not so mournfully on me below;
You freeze my heart with a frenzied fear,
   You fill my soul with a fearful woe.
You drive me mad when I see you shine;
   Avaunt from the sky with your goblin glow!
You know 'twas the deed of the Demon, Wine—
   'Twas the Demon, Wine, that dealt the blow.

"MAGNA EST VERITAS, ET PRÆVALEBIT."

Let Tyrants teach that "Might makes Right,"
   Let Treason join the canting cry,
Let hireling might e'en win the fight,
   Yet, "Truth is great," and cannot die:
What though the Truth be trodden down,
   What though the holiest cause may fail,
Though Wrong may wear the Victor's crown,
   Yet, "Truth is great, and will prevail."

Not dead the Cause, which millions roused,
   The Cause for which a Nation bled,
The Cause which pious Polk espoused—
   The Cause of Jackson is not dead!
What though the Southern sword be sheathed,
   What though in dust her banners trail,
Immortal Truth is round them wreathed,
   And "Truth is great, and will prevail."

By all the hosts that Lee has led
   To front the vaulting Vandal flood,

By every drop so bravely shed
　　On Antietam's field of blood—
Magruder's charge at Malvern Hill,
　　And Spottsylvania's iron hail,
By all our dead, remember still,
　　That "Truth is great, and will prevail."

And ye, who followed Jackson's form
　　Where only bravest dared to go—
Who watched him in the battle's storm,
　　Like lightning, rend the stubborn foe—
Ay! ye, who never yet did yield—
　　Who never yet were seen to quail
Before the foe, on equal field,
　　Know—"Truth is great, and will prevail."

Then pause, ye Tyrants, and be taught,
　　That trampled Truth will rise again;
Ye cannot bind ethereal thought,
　　That laughs to scorn the Victor's chain.
From old Potomac's classic wave
　　To Rio Grande's historic dale,
A voice from every gory grave
　　Cries—"Truth is great, and will prevail."

See, Hope's bright arch yet spans the cloud,
　E'en while we lay our banners by,
And living Truth shall burst the shroud,
　Which wraps in gloom the Southern sky!
Look up, then, Southrons, from the dust,
　And proudly tell your wondrous tale;
In triumph still, be true to trust,
　For "Truth is great, and will prevail."

www.ingramcontent.com/pod-product-compliance
Lightning Source LLC
Chambersburg PA
CBHW030027030726
47499CB00008B/3146